# A Glorious Day in Hell

# in Hell

## THE DAY JESUS
## DESCENDED INTO HELL

# JOHN EUDY

ISBN 978-1-0980-4494-7 (paperback)
ISBN 978-1-0980-4495-4 (digital)

Christian Faith Publishing, Inc.
832 Park Avenue
Meadville, PA 16335
www.christianfaithpublishing.com

Printed in the United States of America

# CONTENTS

# INTRODUCTION

I wrote this story for two reasons. First, many, including myself, have wondered what may have happened in the three days between the death of Jesus on the cross and his resurrection. Tradition teaches, as is exemplified in the Apostle's Creed, that Jesus descended into the underworld (a.k.a., Hades, Sheol, or Limbo, which is the precipice of hell) to preach the gospel and save the just. It goes without saying that no one, save those already in heaven and God himself, truly knows what Jesus did at that time. Therefore, although this pre-Christian tale is fictional, I have done my best to root it in both biblical and traditional teachings (e.g., Catechism of the Catholic Church).

Second, the idea for the story was born out of a moment of depression or posttraumatic stress disorder (PTSD) I experienced. Anyone familiar with this will know there is a trigger which can bring traumatic experiences back from the past in an instant. During these instances, one's mental and emotional faculties can be "locked up" for a short time. For a brief moment in time, I slipped into a very dark place…and the adversary followed me through the breach. There he accused me of many things and brought me even lower before I finally remembered the saving grace of my Lord, who brought me back to the light of reality. This then, is where the idea for this story was born, of what it might have actually looked like to see the Son of God appear in the darkness of limbo. So, although this fictional tale is set over two thousand years ago, it is my sincere hope that all those dealing with the darkness of depression, PTSD, or the like, see the light of our Lord Christ Jesus in their darkest times and know his saving grace is enough to bring them back to the light.

Lastly, legendary writers such as C. S. Lewis or Dante Alighieri, and even modern writers like Tim LaHaye and Jerry B. Jenkins, have used fictional tales to present Christianity from a different perspective, to convey Christian principles and traditions, or even to bring Christian prophesy to life in a modern setting. I too am using fiction to bring about feelings of awe at the sheer power and glory of Jesus Christ, while also giving hope in the love and forgiveness he offers us. Therefore, it is my sincere wish that anyone who reads this tale might renew their sense of discovery and hope in our Lord.

# CHAPTER 1

# A Soldier's Descent

I stood there in shock, staring down at my own dead body, which was still clutching a Roman legion's standard. An arrow had pierced my armor at the seam and plunged into my heart. I looked up and around in bewilderment; it seemed time had stopped. The sights and sounds of the battlefield had vanished. Everything had turned gray, muted, and silent. I staggered backward in disbelief. Drooping my head down to look at my hands, I realized I was completely naked. Why was I not clothed? More importantly, if I was dead, why was I not standing in green fields under a warm sun? A sudden sense of terror seized me.

Without warning, a pair of hot, callous hands grasped my forearms tightly and yanked them behind me. Metal shackles were swiftly and painfully wrapped around my wrists, pinching the skin as a bolt was slid in place to secure them. Before I could turn to see my assailants, a coarse, foul-smelling burlap sack was thrust over my head and pulled tight around my neck. I was then kicked in the back of my knees and forced painfully to the ground. The utter silence finally broken by a growling, guttural laugh, "Heh, heh, heh. Another sinner for the pit!" This was followed by higher-pitched cackling emanating from all around me.

"Chain him to the other one and bring them along!" ordered the deep, snarling voice. I was pulled to my feet and more chains were wrapped around my waist. I could feel the weight of the chain hanging both in front and behind me, weighing on my bare hips. The other soul I had been chained to thrashed in resistance and pulled me backward. The sound of a whip cracking against flesh could be heard, followed by screaming and cursing, and then the weight of the chain pulled again, this time downward. The soul continued to curse when he fell to the ground, calling our captors vile names.

"Get up and get moving!" exclaimed a high-pitched voice, "or you will get another stripe, you worthless sinner!" The chain was yanked from my front and I nearly lost my footing as I lurched forward. My foot struck jagged stone, cutting me. I stumbled, but, not wanting to feel the sting of the whip, kept limping forward in pain. Sorrow supplanted terror as I realized I would not see Elysium; rather, I would be led to Hades and eternal punishment. I began to weep quietly to myself as I wondered what I had done to be cast down so.

I had neither the desire nor the courage to ever take a human life; I just could not bring myself to it. This meant I could never be a true Roman Legionnaire. However, because of my deep desire to serve Rome, I was tasked as a banner carrier when we marched, a cook when we camped, and a laborer when we were tasked with repairing roads or building fortifications. There were a couple of centurions and evocati who were kind and would speak with me after I had served their meal. They would remind me that what we did in life echoed in eternity and encouraged me to find the fortitude to become a fighter before we reached Caesarea Maritima. "Once there," they would say, "we will claim territory, treasure, and slaves in Augustus Caesar's name. The people beyond Hierosolyma[1] will not be submissive either." I, how-ever, had no desire for conquest, only to find the truth of God. Was this lack of courage to fight and to kill what led to my exile to the underworld and eternal punishment? Or was it something worse? Did the one true God I had learned about send me here?

My family in Rome had some land and servants. In my youth, I took pity on our Iudaeus[2] slaves and would occasionally sneak food to them and any old clothing I might happen across. In turn, those slaves taught me many things, specifically Yahweh's commandments and how to follow them. What they believed always struck me as true. Their belief in a living God who loved and cared for them was better than the Roman gods, who seemed to use humanity for their own whims and desires. They also taught me of a coming Messias, one who would save his people from slavery, tyranny, and oppression in this world and in the afterlife.

I would speak with my parents about what they believed in. They would tell me to ignore them and to give no credence to such "nonsense." Still, I began to follow the one true God's commandments, and a hunger for a deeper truth began to grow within me. As I grew older, I tired of being chastised by my father and of arguing with my family over my persistent belief in Yahweh. Once I entered manhood, I thought serving in the Roman army would allow me to expand my knowledge of him and find the truth I was seeking. I thought fortune had smiled upon me when I was assigned to a garrison headed for Hierosolyma itself, which would afford me the opportunity to seek out the truth of God.

---

[1.] Jerusalem (translated from Latin).
[2.] Jewish (translated from Latin).

I learned quickly, though, that as long as I was a Roman soldier, I could never become an open follower of Yahweh. However, I had hoped that privately following his commandments might still bring me close to him when I crossed into the afterlife. I had hoped to walk under the blue sky of his Elysian fields and feel the sun on my face, to experience peace and contentment in his presence. In horrifying contradiction, I found myself weighed down by iron chains and stumbling over the occasional stone on my way to the dominion of hell.

From time to time, I could briefly glimpse my surroundings through holes and gaps in the stinking sackcloth. There was no grass, no trees, no vegetation to be seen. There was no sky, just an ever-darkening atmosphere as we descended what felt like a well-worn stone road. It was as though we descended into a massive chasm where the air became more stale and moist. A strange, but strong, smell of rusting metal permeated the air.

Our procession began to slow, the chains were no longer being pulled, and then our captor bellowed out, "Stoooop, fools." Sandaled footsteps fell heavily on the stone path as he slowly circled around us. "Shall I tell you what the sign over your head reads?" he growled.

The soul behind me shouted, "I don't care what it says, you filthy creature," and he pulled at his chains in defiance.

"Filthy?" the dæmon exclaimed. I could hear him punch the soul, who immediately fell to the ground, pulling me backward again. Moving quickly to my side, the dæmon whispered at my ear, "What about you?" The bag over my head rippled with each exhale of his putrid breath. I did not respond, I only lowered my head and waited for the worst. "Fine!" he snarled. "I will tell you, so you understand your situation."

He began to circle us again, saying in a very slow and even lower snarl, "Though you cannot see them, we are at the iron gates of hell itself. The sign over your head says, 'Abandon all hope ye who enter here.' Heh, heh, heh…" His voice began to rise with excitement. "Welcome to eternal damnation, you pathetic criminals." With that, the clanking sound of iron and the high-pitched grind of rusty metal could be heard as the wide gates opened in the dank cavern. With a yank of the chain and dæmonic laughter, we continued our decent through the gates and into the gaping maw of hell.

We trudged steadily downward on the well-paved and straight road. Soon, water lapping stone could be heard in the distance, broken up occasionally by the sounds of wailing, screaming, and cursing. The smell of rotting flesh filled our nostrils as if thousands of dead fish were decomposing near a shore somewhere. Through the sackcloth, I could just make out dark water moving and glistening in the dim light ahead. I also caught the briefest sight of a large, wooden boat ahead. Wailing and sounds of flesh being smacked with something large grew louder and louder as we neared. Based on legends told around fires at Legionnaire encampments, I assumed it could only have been Charon, the dæmonic ferryman, beating souls with his oar as they boarded his boat to cross the river Styx.

"More for the darkness and fire?" asked Charon as he acknowledged our captors. "Well, throw them in the boat." I was pulled forward by chain and shoved from behind up what must have been the gangplank. Not being able to see, I fell over something unseen and landed on the hard wooden deck. I landed painfully on my shoulder and hit my head on the bare wood, all to the sound of gleeful, dæmonic guffaws. There was no time to regain my senses, though, as I was quickly seized by coarse hands with jagged fingernails and forcefully pulled down inside the hold of the boat. There I was pushed to the side of the hull to make room for more souls, which were soon pressing all around me. The stench of sweat and filth permeated the hold. It wasn't long before I could hear the wooden hatch slam closed above us. Then Charon's oar plunked into the water and the sound of the soul-laden boat's keel scraped the rock on its way back out into the River Styx. We had gotten underway.

My head and shoulders ached and throbbed, my feet bled, and my mind worked to stave off despair. I took the moment to reflect on two things. First, was this how prisoners and slaves were treated after our armies captured them? Some of those who had taught me about the one true God were slaves; did they suffer in this way? My heart broke for them in that moment; them or any who had suffered that way. Secondly, I thought about our captor's words and the sign over the entrance. I couldn't explain it, but I still retained a small spark of hope; I could not give it up. My thoughts kept going back to Yahweh, and I was unable to fully resign myself to an eternity in the underworld. I was once told that my name, Ioannes—or "Yohanan," as the Iudaeus slaves knew me—meant "God is gracious." In my dark silence, I held on to that little flame of hope, hope that maybe God might remember me here and still be gracious to me one day.

The boat pitched and rocked in the turbulent and choppy river currents. Both fear and anger escalated among the souls. Seasickness overcame some, causing them to vomit, creating an even more putrid stench. Although I could not see it, the sounds of physical violence against those seasick souls could be heard in the muffled quiet of that darkened hold. Thankfully, it wasn't a long trip to the other side, and I heard the keel slide up a gravel bank. The boat jolted when it met solid rock, causing us to all heave forward at the sudden stop. Dæmons began gleefully plucking souls from the hold of the boat and brutally casting them ashore. I was no exception. I was drug out of the hold by the chains on my wrists and pushed over the side, where I landed on my bare back on the rocky shore. Feet in the water, head spinning, and my back in pain, I lay there until once again collected by our tormentors and escorted down a coarser road to hell's judgment seat.

Upon arrival, I was unchained from the lead and quickly driven to my knees. Peering through small holes in my sackcloth hood, I could see I was kneeling before a vainglorious dæmon, dressed in the finest Roman robes, a civic crown encircling the two small horns upon his head. He reclined on an ornate curule chair carved from what appeared to be bone. One could easily mistake him for a haughty Roman governor or a pompous senator. "Proceed with your accusations, dæmon," he said with an uninterested sigh.

My captor told this unholy judge how terrible of a soldier I was, how I did nothing in service to my empire but carry a banner and cook meals. "He could not even take one life." He laughed. "He is a coward!" He went on, stating I had not been a good son; disobeying my family's wishes by rejecting Roman gods, associating with Iudaeus slaves, and believing in *their* one true God. "He is a traitor to his family." He accused me of being an "unprofitable servant" to the same living God. "This wretch could not even openly commit to God."

There was a slight pause, and then a sudden sense of guilt overcame me as I realized my other iniquities were about to be laid bare. "The things he did in his youth before attempting to serve his God," the dæmon said, mocking. "Unable to control his hunger, he stole food from a market. Unable to control his lust, he snuck out of his home to visit a lupanar,[3] wantonly laying with women. And, desiring to keep these

---

[3.] Brothel (translated from Latin).

and other sins hidden, he has lied. By his actions, he either allowed, or brought, great evil into the world. Now he thinks God will spare him. No, say I! He deserves punishment."

I could only kneel there in silence. I *was* a liar, a thief, and a fornicator; indeed, the things I had done in my youth had justified my sentence. Still, I held on to that tiny spark of hope; hope that I had done more virtuous things in my adult life, and that the living God might yet find me…even here.

"I agree." The arrogant judge waved his hand dismissively. Then without care, he again sighed, "Take him to Limbo for now. There you can bind him and abandon him until we decide which circle of hell is best suited for him, until he is retrieved by the lower level scum."

The soul chained with me did not think he should be judged when driven to his knees before the court. I heard him curse through clenched teeth at the judge, calling him many names before apparently lunging in the judge's direction. The judge gasped, "You dare?" Our captor grabbed the soul and threw him to the ground, beating him while the judge loudly proclaimed a much worse fate for him.

"Take him to Limbo, for now," the enraged judge declared to our captor. I could hear him rise from his chair and move close to the angry soul. In a vicious tone, he hissed, "I know which circle is suitable for you. I will contact your torturer personally, you disease-ridden criminal. I want to be there when he drags you deeper into hell. You will wait in Limbo in anticipation of our arrival."

He moved back to his comfortable chair and yelled, "Now get him out of my sight and bring the next criminal before me!" Satisfied with the outcome, our captor chained us back together and led us, as a bull is led to slaughter, to our next destination, the darkened world of Limbo.

The smell of sulfur and ash began to overpower the stink of the sackcloth. Everything was growing not just darker, but black in appearance. I couldn't see anything through the shroud over my face. The ground felt hotter on my bare feet, more coarse and jagged. The path had become far more twisting and winding too; it was not the same smooth, wide road that led into hell. About the time I wondered if we were nearing our destination, our captor said in his deep, growling voice, "We are here, slaves." That, however, was about the extent of his courtesy as he immediately shoved me to the ground on my belly and stepped on my back with one foot, making it hard to breathe. I could feel the chain from my shackles being connected to an eye anchored in the black, gritty rock I lay upon. Once chained, the dæmon loosened my hood, removed his foot from my back, and then painfully yanked the sackcloth off my head. I rolled to my side and glanced up to finally see my imprisoner, only to be struck in the face with the back of his hand. He then spat upon my face with the foulest-smelling saliva.

Keeping one eye closed, so the spittle would not run into it, I glanced at the creature with my other eye. His black skin appeared to shimmer blue in the dim light as he stood over me. Red irises blazed through otherwise black eyes. His battle-scarred face twisted with a grotesque, haughty smile. There was a whip ready in his right hand and a large, cruel-looking single-blade axe in the other. He wore dark-brown barbarian armor, with a black, spiked pauldron[4] on his left shoulder. Small blue horns protruded around his bald head, as if it were a twisted crown. His appearance would strike fear in the bravest of warriors I knew.

Through that grotesque smile, he hissed, "You think you lived a virtuous life, did you not?" A deep, guttural chortle slipped past the yellowish, daggerlike teeth set in his blue-

---

4. Armor plate for shoulder.

and-black distorted face. "You are a sinner. God does not love you, worm." With a sudden swift motion, he cracked his whip, and I felt the searing pain run down my side and back, splitting my skin. Ash stirred up from the whip, immediately mingled with my blood, and burned.

Through fear and torment, I could feel hopelessness creep into my mind, and I wailed in pain, "Deus meus[5], why have you forsaken me here?"

"Shut up," scolded the dæmon in contempt. "God is the one who sent you here, fool." Then he swiftly kicked me in the head. "We told you to abandon hope, wretch. Go ahead, then, despair, for you are a great sinner who does not deserve to be in the presence of God." He then ground his hot, sandaled foot into the open cut on my side, making it open further and burn more fiercely. "You will never have any rest or sleep. There is no peace for you here." He laughed with hearty satisfaction and all the other, smaller dæmons skulking about in the shadows joined in with their incessant cackling. All I could do was curl up on the bare, black stone, shackles cutting into my wrists and falling embers stinging my naked body.

The dæmon said, "Bah! Leave him to his despair." He then turned his attention to the other soul. A malevolent grin spread across his face. He motioned for the smaller dæmons to bind the soul to the ground and remove his hood. He then placed his axe on the ground and secured his whip to his side while they carried out his order. As soon as his hood had been removed, and without warning, our captor unleashed his fury on the unnamed soul.

Breathing heavily from delivering his savage assault, the dæmon finally stood upright and took a step back. "Truly, I

---

[5.] "My God" (translated from Latin).

16

enjoyed that." he said as he reached for his axe. Though still conscious, the unnamed soul lay limp on the ground. Satisfied in our humiliation, our captor motioned to his band of dæmons to leave, saying, "Come, let us find more sinners like these." He chuckled ominously before finally departing.

I lay there in the blackness for a moment, my body racked with pain. Finally, I wiped the blood, spittle, and ash from my swollen eye, and then painfully rose to my knees to survey my surroundings. There was no sky, just black, stale air. The rock, too, appeared black. The only light came from the red-orange glow of what looked like lava flows emanating from a lake of fire or cauldron of magma near a vast chasm. There were no stars in the darkened sky, just billowing, gray clouds moving about like a shadowy, turbulent thunderstorm. Glowing embers and big flakes of gray ash fell sporadically from the ebony tempest. The landscape reminded me of a slowly erupting volcano seen just after dusk.

I looked at the soul chained near me but could only see his back in the firelight. He twisted and turned in agony and rage as a large, burning ember landed on him. He cursed through gnashed teeth as the ember burned his flesh. Though he thrashed about with rage, I pitied him in his agony. Who knew how long we were to stay there, how long until we were dragged deeper into the pit? "Deus meus, salva mea,"[6] I humbly whispered to myself.

---

[6.] "My God, save me" (translated from Latin).

# CHAPTER 2

# The Appearance

Time passed, but I knew not how much. My naked body was covered in small cuts, bruises, blisters, and sores. How long had I been chained there listening to sounds of violence, of screams, of wailing and weeping? The distant lake of fire churned and sent embers into the black, turbulent sky, which later fell and burned my bare skin. There was no water in that scorched, volcanic landscape. My lips had already split, cracked, and burned. My throat was parched, not even my own saliva could ease the dryness when I swallowed. I had only been given enough chain to either sit up or rise to my bruised knees; I could not stand. The abandonment, the torment, the pain, it was maddening. The temptation to despair, to resign myself to this darkness, weighed heavy on my mind. Thoughts of hopelessness, that there was truly no way out of this place, constantly seeped into my mind. How long had this been going on? Had I been there days, months, years? There was no knowing in the scope of eternity.

I looked over at the soul chained near me. Not only was he sitting upright, but he had turned toward me so I could see him more clearly. He seemed to be peering through me to some far-off place. His face and body looked far worse than mine. Marks and scars long prior to coming here covered his face and torso; it looked as though he had suffered much in life. I wondered if he had been a slave or a warrior. I asked, "How long do you think we've been here, friend?"

His head turned slightly, and his intense focus landed on me. "I'm not your friend!" he screamed at me through clenched teeth. "Were you not listening? We've been sent here for eternity. Time no longer matters. Stultus!7"

"I know, I know," I said sadly. "I cannot explain why, but I had hoped the one true God, or his Messias, might still save me—well, us, before we descended any further."

"You have hope?" he snorted in derision. "You're even dumber that I thought. I would kick you myself if I could reach you! Shut up and leave me alone." He turned his body and fixed his gaze on the black pit in the distance.

I turned back to observe my bleak surroundings, wondering if, or when, the remnant of hope I held on to might give out. When might I give in to the despair and madness of that place? Then, without any explanation, I was granted sight of events unfolding on the earth above.

I saw a man kneeling in a garden at night. He prayed to the one true God, whom he called his Father, with his entire being, sweating blood in his agony. Soon after his prayers were complete, he was betrayed by one of his own friends. He was arrested and beaten as the rest of his band of brothers fled. He was led by chains to different places and brought before different authorities, an unruly court, an egotistical governor, and a would-be king. Each time he appeared before them was a mockery. Somehow, I knew nothing he was accused of was truth; it was lies and half-truths, I could feel it. He broke his silence so seldom, and, when he did, his

---

7. Fool (translated from Latin).

claims were consistently rejected as either foolish or blasphemous. He was finally condemned by the weak and selfish governor who cared not for truth but only for power over the mob who brought him. There, in the darkness, I begin to wonder whether what I heard and saw, including the man's claims to be the Son of God, were true; whether this could truly be the Messias I was taught about.

Again, I saw the innocent man suffer, scourged, and beaten. I learned quickly that I was not the only one to have this vision. Each time he was marked with the whip, each time he was struck, an uproar came from dæmons and evil souls scattered throughout the darkness all around me. The roar was as loud as a packed coliseum. *Who is this man,* I think to myself, *that he would endure such abuse for those he called friends, brothers, sisters? Who is he that dæmons would cheer so at his torture?*

Then we saw a band of dishonorable soldiers hide him away after the scourging, torturing him by brutally fixing a crown of thorns on his head and mocking him by bowing to him. A dæmon somewhere near me in the ash-filled darkness squealed with giddy, "These are my kind of soldiers." My only thoughts were, *How much more can this man, this Son of God, take? He did nothing to deserve this!* Dæmons can be heard chanting for his crucifixion, when a sudden hush fell over Limbo.

The man who turned him over in the garden had despaired of his treacherous act and hung himself. Now all eyes turned to watch the soul of this traitor descend into hell, hanging in the air from the noose he had tied himself. With an eerie, flame-colored spotlight on him, the hanged man descended through the dusky, ash-filled air, down into the distant pit. For this traitor, it was clear there would be no stopping until he reached the very bottom. Dæmons and sinners alike hissed, threw stones at him, and shouted "Traitor!"

He could not wail or scream because of the noose tied tightly around his throat, but he did gnash his teeth and flail about wildly as he tried to defend himself from the stones. He quickly slipped into the depths of the chasm near the lake of fire and was out of sight. It was then that a raucous cheer went up, as though some gladiator had just won a great victory. "Guilty!" they all screamed.

I watched as this Jesus was given a full cross to carry. Such a heavy burden. He stumbled when being led out to his death as I did in my journey to Limbo. He was whipped, beaten, and suffered the same pains and more on his journey. Upon his arrival to Iocus Calvariæ,[8] he was stripped of his garments, nearly as naked as I. He was placed on his back atop his cross lying on the ground. I knew what came next, but I could not bear to watch it. I fell prostrate on the hot, black rock and buried my face in my hands. I could not watch as the carpenter raised his hammer.

The subsequent ping of hammer on nail resonated through bare landscape of hell, echoing off the volcanic terrain and inciting the dæmons to a disgusting ecstatic cry. They shouted out in frenzy with each hammer blow, while I bitterly wept with sorrow with each one. "No, stop this! He does not deserve this!" I shouted. An unseen dæmon rushed out of the black wasteland and kicked me in the side, knocking the wind out of me.

"Shut up, sinner!" he exclaimed in his bloodlust.

While I had watched the suffering of Jesus, I had forgotten my own agony for a time, but now the pain in my ribs was nearly unbearable. Still, I caught my breath and lifted my tear-filled eyes in time to see him raised up on his cross. He was flanked by criminals on their own crosses. One mocked

---

8. Place of the Skulls, a.k.a., Calvary (translated from Latin).

Jesus and his claim to be the Messias. The other proclaimed his own punishment as just, and simply asked the Son of God to remember him when he came into his kingdom. Through his own pain, Jesus lovingly forgave the repentant criminal, promising him paradise. My heart gave a sudden, hard beat and that flicker of hope I had held on to warmed in my chest. *It must be the Messias*, I thought.

Jesus then uttered a loud cry and breathed his last; he died on the cross. At that, a great roar went up as loud as twenty coliseums filled to capacity, all cheering at once. To dæmon and evil soul alike, seeing the Son of God perish on the cross was a glorious day in hell. However, all became silent and still immediately afterward; a great hush unexpectedly blanketed all of hell. Only the churning, crackling fires could be heard.

A distant thunderclap boomed, and then rumbled across the muffled black sky, breaking the terrible silence. I looked up to see a point of pure, white light twinkling above the volcanic maelstrom. It burned brighter than any star in the night sky I could remember, brighter than any flash of lightning or burning ember. It began to grow bigger into the shape of a giant round orb. At first, the white-and-yellow orb appeared like the sun as seen through an ash cloud of an erupting volcano. It was encircled by a spinning band of golden fire, sparking as it spun around the orb. This flickering band released a great wind which blew the gray clouds away from the light in all directions. Then, in the bright round circle of white light, there appeared a figure, the silhouette of a man, dark against the light. He stood upright with his hands extended outward from his sides. I could not make out other details of this figure, but deep in my heart, I felt the flame of hope warm my chest.

The appearance of the figure in the light sent all of Limbo into panic. All around me were the sudden sounds of fearful scurrying about like a field of rats trying to hide from a great, golden hawk. Out of the chasm, a deep roar erupted in opposition to the light. It shook the very ground I was chained to. The deafening voice, filled with rage, defiance, and contempt, bellowed, "No, Son of God, these souls are mine! I will not part with a single one!"

From the silhouette in the light came a calm, soft voice full of authority. "Silence. You will have only what my Father wills you to have. I am here only for the just who went to sleep before I had come. I am their shepherd, and they will know my voice, for I am the way, the truth, and the life." At that, the soul next to me, and all of Limbo, by the sound of it, bent a knee to the Son of God. All was again silent as he had commanded it.

With a great explosion, the most brilliant white light with gold all around its fringes burst from the orb. The gold fringe appeared to shimmer, sparkle, and crackle, before expanding outward and descending all around. I quickly realized it was not just an ordinary shimmering light. Each flickering light was an angel, each one sent out to find the just in Limbo. As the brilliant legion descended in all directions, I noticed the figure too began to change and grow in appearance. Though his silhouette was still dark, I could see light shining through holes in his hands and feet, and I knew at that moment who the figure was. Then something unexpected began to happen.

It was hard to tell at first, but it looked as if he were coming toward me. *How could this be? Surely, I was not worthy of the Messias, the Son of God*, I thought. I watched him approach long enough to see he was clothed in the purest white linen and he stood on a billowing white cloud, which gracefully descended toward me. My heart pounded faster with both fear and hope. Why should I be so blessed by his presence? From my knees, I bowed my head, and, keeping it down, I murmured, "Surely I am not worthy of he who conquers death."

On his knees and holding his head up with false pride, the voice of the nameless soul next to me said, "Shut up, stultus! Don't you recognize the adversary? All this light is only a trick to lull you in. He is Lucifer, the Morning Star. Don't be tricked by his light or his appearance. Our time has come. He is here to take us deeper into the pit, to greater punishment. Don't trust him!"

Then just as softly as a devoted father speaks with love to his young child, the Messias spoke, "Ioannes." I shuttered and began to cry in utter joy at the sound of his pure voice. Still hiding my face in my ash-covered hands, I responded with fear and humility, "I am here, Lord."

Though there were no footsteps to be heard, and rightfully so, as this forsaken place was not worthy that the Son of God should set foot in it, I felt the figure draw near. His light and power were overwhelming in that dark place of evil. I removed my hands from my face and clasped them together tightly at my chest hoping this was truly the Messias, the Son of the living God. As I felt him draw near, I managed to say through parched throat and split lips, "Domine miserere nobis.[9] Please have mercy."

Though I thought it impossible, my heart actually beat faster, thumping against my chest so hard I thought it might burst out. My body, still racked with much pain, ached with the rush of blood coursing through it with each pounding beat. Tears poured from my eyes, making my face a black, muddy mess. It was hard to breathe and sob at the same time; my body trembled. *Dare I lift my eyes upward?* I thought. Without warning, his soft yet strong hand touched my

---

[9.] "Lord have mercy" (translated from Latin).

shoulder, and everything changed in an instant…a calming peace pushed fear from me. I no longer trembled. I was still. I could breathe.

"My child," came the soft, sweet voice "I know you. I have seen all you have done in belief of my Father, the one true and living God. Though they were prisoners, slaves, you gave food and clothing to the ones who taught you my Father's commandments, and of my coming. From then on, I watched you seek out the truth. Although you may not have known, it was me you sought, me you fed, me you clothed, and me you served. You have seen my passion and my sacrifice. You have cried out for me, and now, I am here for you. Will you trust in me? Will my grace be enough for you? Will you have faith in me as the Son of God? Do you accept the gift of salvation I offer?"

With my head still bowed, I answered humbly, "Though I have been no servant of thine, my Lord, and am not worthy of you, yes, still, I will trust in you. Your grace is more than enough for me. Truly, you are the Messias, the Son of God, and I humbly receive you."

He drew a slow, steady breath, and then gently exhaled, breathing on me. I could feel his sweet-smelling breath move through the hair on my head and down my back. His gentle breath blew soot and ash from my body. The chains fell from my wrists, which were still clasped tightly together at my chest. My throat was no longer parched. My burns, wounds, and bruises disappeared; my skin was cleansed and made whole. I felt all pain leave my body and my soldier's strength return to me.

After this, I heard the rush of enormous wings, hovering just above my left shoulder. They beat rhythmically, making a whooshing sound with each flap. The wind from those giant wings blew away the ash and filth from all around my prostrated body. Then I heard sandaled footsteps light on the ground just near my left and the beating wings stop; one of the many angels previously seen descending brilliantly in the dark sky had landed next to me. He reached down, lifted me to my feet, and then immediately clothed me in a pale blue robe with a golden sash around my waist.

I opened my eyes to that brilliant light, and, lifting them up slightly, was greeted by the Messias, the man on the cross, the Son of God…Jesus. His eyes, looking down on me with unfathomable love, blazed forth in a deep copper color, as though they were molten metal. Divine light seemed to emanate from his face, his entire being. An overwhelming sense of undeniable joy filled my heart and soul and I could not stop the wide smile that spread across my face. Jesus smiled back. "The hope you clung to has been rewarded, Ioannes. Your faith has saved you."

He raised his arms to embrace me and I could clearly see the holes in his hands out of the corner of my eye. Bending down slightly as a father does for his child, he lovingly embraced me and softly said, "Well done, my good and faithful servant." Tears of unbridled joy flowed freely from my eyes, and, like a child, I happily returned his warm embrace. I could feel his love and warmth move through me, filling my heart with everlasting bliss.

He released me, and, with his hands still on my shoulders, continued to smile at me. "I still have much to accomplish here, and in the world above, Ioannes. Go now, to paradise with you. Great joy awaits you there. We will meet again, very soon, after I have fully accomplished my Father's work. You must go further up and further into my kingdom to find me again."

With a last pat on my shoulder and an encouraging smile, he turned to move throughout that forsaken precipice to the abyss, claiming others as he had claimed me. I could not remove the smile from my face as I watched him in awe.

The angel at my side also smiled. Together we watched evil souls and dæmons alike flee as the Magnificent One brought ever-expanding light to Limbo and joy to those who awaited his coming, those who dared to hope in his salvation.

"I am Præsidiel. Come, my friend," said the angel, "as the Lord said, it is time to leave this horrid place." He stretched out his white wings, which reflected the holy light of Jesus, and for the first time I noticed his deep-blue leather breastplate trimmed in gold. His armor was set against a light-gray tunic with a golden belt wrapping his waist. A golden scabbard held his gladius at his side. His caligae[10] were the same golden color as his belt and the trim on his armor. He appeared physically to be a perfect copy of man, but some-how more elegant. He took my hand and gestured to rise. We began to ascend toward the perfect orb of light. The sound of his massive wings beating near me were comforting.

As I looked about, I saw thousands of similar angels rising into the light with us. They all accompanied other souls. In the darkness of hell, they appeared as glinting points of light, but as we moved closer together and into the light of the orb, it was easy to see those the Son of God had come for: Adam, Eve, his servants and prophets of old, as well as others who had believed in and followed the one true God.

Some would call us the just pagans of the world; me, I was simply happy to have been called by him at all. Truly, I was contented in being called one of his. I then realized I would need all of eternity to properly express my thankfulness to be counted among them, to express my eternal gratitude for the sacrifice, mercy, and grace of our Lord Jesus, the Christ. My meager faith and undying hope had been rewarded; by his sacrificial love I had been redeemed!

---

10. A soldier's sandals (translated from Latin).

It had not been the moment of his death on the cross, rather it was this moment, the moment of the Messias's appearance in hell, the salvation of those God still loved, the ascension of the just into his kingdom, *this* moment is what made that day a *truly* glorious day in hell.

I marveled at how vast the chasm between the threshold of light and Limbo was; it increased quickly and immensely as we ascended. I looked back one final time with pity on those still there. There I saw the nameless soul, who had journeyed with me, being drug by a horrible creature to the edge of the chasm. The pompous dæmon who had judged us both followed at his side, antagonizing him, striking him, and spitting on him. The nameless man's fate had been sealed by a life poorly lived and his utter rejection of the Messias.

I turned back to face the oscillating orb of light. Everything changed as we passed through it. No more sounds of violence, wailing, or erupting fire could be heard. No darkness was to be seen. No rancid odors or smell of sulfur. As soon as we passed through the brilliant threshold, we landed on solid ground. The soft, green grass pleasantly tickled my still bare feet. My angel, folding his wings, and continuing to smile at me, said, "Welcome to paradise, Ioannes."

"Thank you, my friend." Then I closed my eyes and lifted my face to the sky, soaking in the warmth of it for a moment. Opening my eyes, I slowly surveyed the lush, sprawling domain. Fields of tall grasses, meadows filled with many kinds of flowers, and deep green forests with fruit-bearing trees of all kinds surrounded the wide, rolling hills. Streams of the clearest water flowed down from vast, snowcapped mountains rising up from behind the forests and wound in various directions, while fresh, cool breezes carried floral scents throughout the wide lands of heaven. Even the fabled Elysian fields could not compare to this.

In the distance, a great gleaming city sat majestically upon a hill. Its tan and white stone buildings beckoned new arrivals to wander its sacred streets, to explore them with the blessed. Millions of stars, and even other worlds, stretched out in the sky beyond the luminous city. No matter which way I looked, all lands, distant or near, could be seen clearly as if they were but a short walk away. Some places were easily recognizable while others I knew not.

All of creation had not only been remade but was laid out before me. The prospect of finding and knowing Jesus in this place was more than exhilarating. There would be no more darkness, no more weeping and gnashing of teeth, no more death and despair. Life, love, truth, and joyous discovery was before me as he promised.

I turned to the angel next to me who had easily read the unbridled joy and curiosity on my face. He tilted his head in a slight bow and motioned with his hand as if he were releasing me into this holy realm. I nodded back in gratitude, while lightly striking my breast in salute, and then took my first step into the kingdom of heaven. It was time to seek out my magnificent Saviour; it was time to go further up and further into his glorious kingdom…

# ABOUT THE AUTHOR

Johnathan Eudy is a twenty-six-year military veteran. He enlisted on Pearl Harbor Day in 1988 and subsequently completed five years in the Army National Guard before transitioning over to the U. S. Coast Guard and serving another twenty-one years. He is a rare, two-time graduate of basic training, has served on both sides of a levee during flood operations (levee building with the Army and patrolling flooded areas with the Coast Guard), and is a graduate of US Army's Sapper School and the Coast Guard's Chief Petty Officer's Academy. John has lived in five states and visited forty other states and territories, including Guam. He retired from military service in 2015.

After the military, John took on civilian roles in human resources as a recruiter and HR coordinator. He subsequently left HR in 2019 to not only pursue personal interests, including his dream of becoming a published author, but also to become a stay-at-home dad for his two daughters. John and his family currently reside in their native Missouri. He has been married to his lovely wife for twenty-five years, and they are the proud parents of four children, two of whom are already with God in heaven.

CPSIA information can be obtained
at www.ICGtesting.com
Printed in the USA
LVHW011720040920
664825LV00007B/453